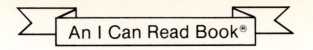
An I Can Read Book®

Zack's Alligator

by Shirley Mozelle

Pictures by
James Watts

HarperCollins*Publishers*

This book is a presentation of Newfield Publications, Inc.
Newfield Publications offers book clubs for children
from preschool through high school. For further
information write to: **Newfield Publications, Inc.,**
4343 Equity Drive, Columbus, Ohio 43228.

Published by arrangement with HarperCollins Publishers.
Newfield Publications is a federally registered trademark of
Newfield Publications, Inc.
I Can Read Book is a registered trademark of
HarperCollins Publishers.

Zack's Alligator

Library of Congress Cataloging-in-Publication Data
Mozelle, Shirley.

Zack's Alligator.

(An I can read book)
Summary: When Zack soaks his new alligator keychain
in water, it grows into a full-sized and fun-loving alligator.
[1. Alligators—Fiction] I. Watts, James,
1955-   ill. II. Title.   III. Series.
PZ7.M868Za 1989 [E] 88-32069
ISBN 0-06-024309-0
ISBN 0-06-024310-4 (lib. bdg.)

For Sally, Nancy, Nina—
and Uncle Alfred

A big box came in the mail for Zack.

It was from Zack's uncle Jim

in Florida.

Zack shook the box.

What could it be? he wondered.

He untied the bow

and ripped off the paper.

There was another box inside.

Zack lifted the lid.

Inside was an alligator key chain,

with a note from Uncle Jim.

It said,

DEAR ZACK,
HERE IS A PRESENT
FOR YOU.
HAVE FUN!
LOVE,
YOUR UNCLE JIM
P.S. WATER BRIDGET.

Zack held up the key chain.

"This must be Bridget," he said.

Zack put Bridget in the sink

and turned on the faucet.

Bridget began to move—

her head turned,

her tail curled.

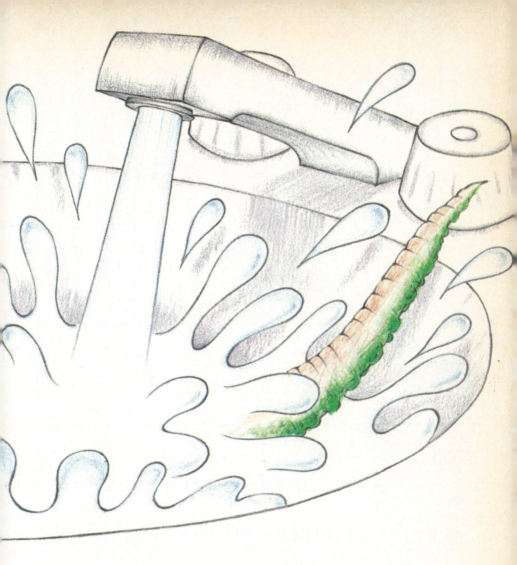

Bridget grew bigger

and bigger.

Soon she filled the sink.

Zack moved Bridget to the tub

and turned on the shower.

Bridget stretched and sighed.

"That feels *so* good!" she said.

Zack watched.

12

Bridget grew larger

and l a r g e r.

She grew out of the tub

and over the side.

Bridget moaned and groaned

and whipped her tail.

She splashed water everywhere.

"What is going on in there?"

called Zack's mother.

"I am watering the alligator,"

said Zack.

"Alligator! What alligator?"

"The one Uncle Jim sent," Zack said.

He heard his mother laugh.

"I see," she said.

"Well, clean up when you are done."

"I will," said Zack.

Bridget crawled out of the tub

and onto the floor.

"I am hungry," she said.

"Do you have any fish?"

"I don't know," said Zack.

"Let's go see."

Bridget followed Zack
down the stairs
and into the kitchen.

Zack opened the refrigerator door.

"No fish?" said Bridget.

"No," said Zack. "No fish.

But here is some meat loaf.

I can fix you a Meat Loaf Special!"

"What is that?" asked Bridget.

"A surprise," said Zack.

"I love surprises!" said Bridget.

19

Bridget went into the living room

and stretched out on the sofa.

The sofa shook.

Bridget looked at the TV.

20

"What a funny-looking box!"

she said.

Then she hollered to Zack,

"Hurry up with the food!"

"I am coming!" said Zack.

21

He was making

his Meat Loaf Special—

meat loaf, peanut butter,

mustard, banana,

and a couple of pickles.

"Zack, what are you doing?"

asked his mother.

"I am fixing some meat loaf

for Bridget."

"Who is Bridget?"

"The alligator," said Zack.

"Oh, of course," said Mother.

"Well, save some for dinner."

"I will," said Zack.

Bridget ate every bite

of Zack's Meat Loaf Special.

"Delicious!" she said.

"I have never eaten anything

like that before.

Back home in the Glades,

I eat mostly fish

and snakes and slugs."

Suddenly Bridget jumped up

from the sofa.

"Time for a walk," she said.

Bridget wobbled to the door.

26

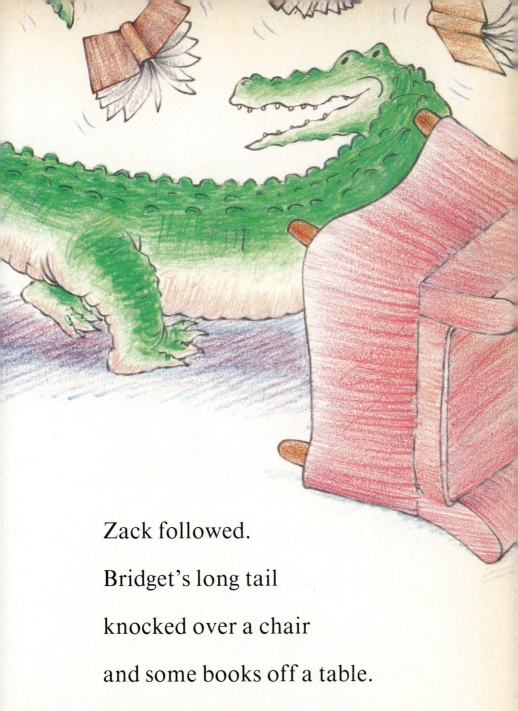

Zack followed.

Bridget's long tail

knocked over a chair

and some books off a table.

Zack picked up the chair

and the books.

"We are going out, Mom," he called.

"We?" she asked.

"Oh, yes, you and Bridget.

I forgot.

Well, don't be too long.

Dad will be home soon."

Outside, Bridget was wrestling

with the garden hose.

"I will get you!" she growled.

She gave the hose a big bite.

Water squirted everywhere.

Zack ran to turn off the water.

"That snake will not bother anyone

ever again!" said Bridget.

Zack sighed and shook his head.

Bridget took off down the sidewalk.

Zack followed.

Just then the mailman

pulled up in his truck.

"What is that?" cried Bridget.

Before Zack could answer,

Bridget attacked!

She bit the tire of the truck.

Air hissed out.

"Dogs are bad enough,"

shouted the mailman,

"but I cannot handle this.

No, sir! Not alligators!"

The mailman jumped into his truck

and drove away with a flat tire.

Klump! Klump! Klump!

Bridget shook her head.

"I am glad we don't have those

in the Glades," she said.

Zack tried to say something,

but Bridget was off again.

They came to the park.

Bridget wanted to swing.

After that,

she climbed the monkey bars.

Then she jumped on the seesaw.

Zack had never seen anyone

seesaw by herself.

Next, Bridget ran

to the merry-go-round.

Round and round she went.

Bridget began to sing.

"Oh, I am a gator from the Glades,

and I can do anything—

and I mean anything!"

41

Bridget got so dizzy,

she fell off the merry-go-round.

Zack helped Bridget up.

Just then his best friend, Turk,

rode up on his bicycle.

"Hey, Zack!" said Turk.

"Where did you get that alligator?"

"From my uncle Jim," said Zack.

"Some uncle!" Turk said.

Suddenly Bridget shouted,

"What's that fuzzy-wuzzy?"

The woman took one look at Bridget

and picked up her dog.

"Come on, Poopsie," she said.

"Let Mama take you home."

Bridget did a cartwheel.

"Who would want

that fuzzy-wuzzy anyway?" she said.

"I am thirsty, not hungry."

45

Bridget did a quick one-two,

and hop-skipped to the fountain.

She drank big gulps of water.

Zack and Turk watched.

"Will you bring Bridget to school?"

asked Turk.

"I don't know," said Zack.

A policeman came over.

"You need a leash

for that alligator," he said.

"There is a law, you know!"

"Yes, sir," said Zack.

The policeman frowned.

"Well, keep him under control."

"*Him*?" cried Bridget.

"Well, I beg his pardon!

How rude!

Hasn't he ever seen

a girl gator before?"

"You should bring her to school,"

said Turk.

"Maybe," said Zack.

Zack and Turk rode Bridget

around the park.

50

Suddenly Bridget started to shrink.

"I need more water," she said.

Zack and Turk helped her

to the fountain.

Bridget slurped the cool water.

"This place is too dry," she said.

"In the Glades,

there is plenty of water

and moss and tall grass."

"What are the Glades?" asked Turk.

"The Everglades," said Zack.

"They are in Florida,

where my uncle Jim lives."

"Do you think

he could send me an alligator?"

asked Turk.

"I don't know," said Zack.

"I will ask him."

"That would be great!" said Turk.

54

"We have to go now," said Zack.

"Don't forget to bring Bridget

to school!" yelled Turk.

"Oh, please!" Bridget said to Zack.

"I want to see what school is like!"

"We will see," said Zack.

On the way home,

Bridget was shrinking more and more.

She looked up at Zack

with big, shiny alligator eyes.

"Will you water me again?" she asked.

"I will water you every day,"

said Zack.

"Good!" said Bridget.

Bridget was getting smaller

and smaller.

She bobbed her head up and down

and began singing.

"I am a gator from the Glades,

and I like to have fun every day.

Oh, yeah!"

When they got home,

Bridget was key chain size.

Zack put her safely in his pocket.

"Hello," said Zack's father.

"Your mother said

you were out with the alligator.

May I see it?"

"Yes, sir," said Zack.

Zack pulled out the key chain

with a small alligator

hanging from it.

"That's very nice," said his father.

"Now go wash up for dinner."

Zack went upstairs to his room.

He could hear

his mother tell his father

they would have chicken for dinner

instead of meat loaf.

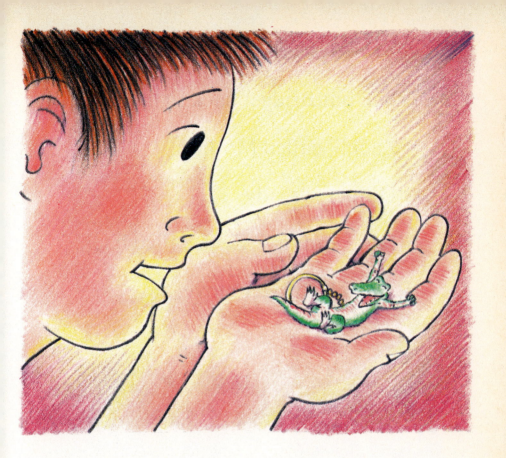

"Are you all right?" whispered Zack.

"Never better," Bridget said.

She yawned.

"Don't forget to water me tomorrow."

"I won't," said Zack.

Zack put Bridget back in his pocket.

"Zack!" called Mother.

"Dinner is ready."

"I am coming!" Zack called back.

Zack felt Bridget move.

He patted his pocket

and smiled.

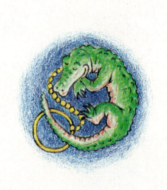